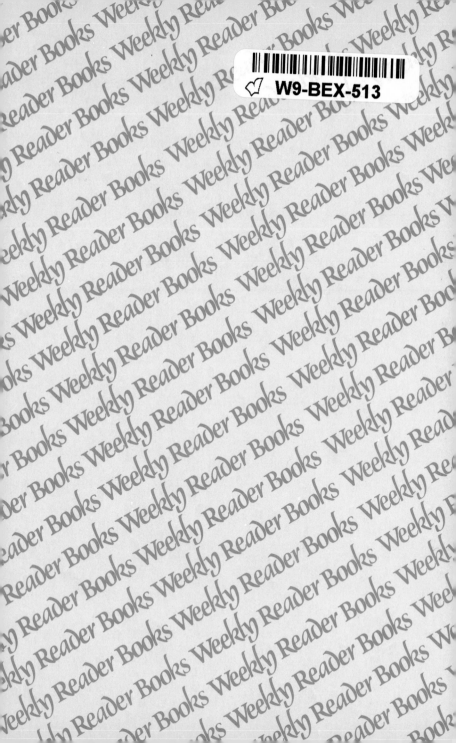

Some Friend!

I don't know why I'm the one who always has to give in. Well, yes I do know. As far as I'm concerned it's Rob or no one. He's been my best friend since we were six.

Sometimes it's hard for Mike to stay friends with Rob, who always has to have things his way. Mike persists because he doesn't feel the same closeness with Kenny or Bubba or any of the other guys in his class.

Mike envies Rob's nerve and his ability to manipulate others. Rob is the kind of natural salesman who can con people into buying things even when they don't want them. He even cons Mike into selling greeting cards with him door-to-door.

One day, though, Rob pushes Mike too far and they get into a serious fistfight. The fight makes Mike realize that he must take a stand of his own with Rob if he wants to keep his self-respect.

In her first novel for young readers, Carol Carrick sensitively portrays the ups and downs of a preteen friendship. Mike's hopes and frustrations will be instantly recognized by anyone who has ever had a friend like Rob.

CAROL CARRICK

Weekly Reader Books presents

Some Friend!

pictures by Donald Carrick

Houghton Mifflin/Clarion Books/New York

Houghton Mifflin/Clarion Books
52 Vanderbilt Avenue, New York, NY 10017

Text copyright © 1979 by Carol Carrick
Pictures copyright © 1979 by Donald Carrick

Library of Congress Cataloging in Publication Data
Carrick, Carol.   Some friend!
SUMMARY: Mike has always been a little in awe of his
self-assertive friend Rob but one day, when pushed too far,
Mike realizes he will have to take a stand of his own or lose
self-respect.
[1. Friendship—Fiction] I. Carrick, Donald. II. Title.
PZ7.C2344So [Fic]   79-11490   ISBN 0-395-28966-1

For Bob Donmoyer

In kindergarten I had a friend, Ryan, who played with me every day. When he moved away I missed him a lot. I remember we both cried when we had to say good-bye to each other.

Then I noticed Rob. He was there in my class all along, but I'd never thought anything about him. He's been my best friend ever since.

chapter 1

Rob and I had been carrying the cardboard box around all afternoon. It was like summer already, except school wasn't out yet. Luckily we lived in the old part of Stony Brook, which is like a village, with lots of big trees. It wasn't so hot if we stuck to the shady streets.

The next house was going to be mine. I took a deep breath, put the box down on the front steps, and knocked on the door. It didn't sound very loud, so I had to knock again, harder this time. I looked at Rob and raised my eyebrows. This was always the worst part, waiting to see what kind of person would answer.

A young man opened the door. He must have been watching a ball game because I could hear it on the television set behind him. He looked like a nice guy, so I plunged right in.

"Hi. We're selling greeting cards and stationery. Would you like to buy some?"

"Sorry," the man said. "My wife isn't here."

I took off my baseball cap and wiped my sweaty face with my arm. I hadn't made a sale all afternoon. I must have looked disappointed because the man said good-naturedly, "All right. Let's see what you've got."

I fumbled in the cardboard box, looking for something that might appeal to him, but I kept coming up with stuff like "Scented Florals" and index cards with "Recipe Treasures from the Kitchen of . . ." printed on them.

"How about our all-purpose greeting assortment?" I asked, holding up the box.

Just as he was about to take it, there was a roar from the television crowd and the announcer was screaming, "It's a long drive to center field!"

The man spun around toward the set. "Get it! Get it!" he yelled. "Oh, no! What's the matter with you?"

After he'd finished chewing out the center fielder, he noticed that Rob and I were still standing on his front steps.

"Um . . ." he said, flapping his hands and looking from us to the television set.

"I guess we better come back another time," I said feebly.

"Yeah, yeah," the man agreed, relaxing. "Come back tomorrow. My wife will be here then." And he disappeared into the gloom of the living room.

"You could've sold that guy a box of cards easy, Mike," Rob said, sounding annoyed. "He would have bought something just to get rid of us. Some salesman! You talked him right out of it."

Rob had seen the cards and stationery advertised in a magazine and sent away for a box of samples. He'd made me his business partner. For every box of something we sold, we got points toward a prize. Rob

had a catalog with pictures of all the things we could save up for.

"You're good at it, Rob," I said. "But I feel dumb when I try to sell people stuff, banging on their door, asking them to buy something they don't want. What're they supposed to say?"

"They can say no. We're not twisting their arm."

"Go away, little boy," I said, imitating the shaky voice of an old lady. "I'm against kids trying to earn money. Why don't you stop bothering me and hold up a supermarket or something?"

Rob snickered. "See, that's right! We're giving our customers a chance to do their civic duty and keep kids like us out of jail. Besides, they're getting a good deal."

He grabbed my arm. "C'mon, let's try just one more house. Watch me. I bet I get us at least 75 points with this sale."

Rob rang the bell. There was an eruption of barks inside and a skinny woman with a sour look answered the door. I'd have said she was the "sorry, not interested" type. Rob turned on the winning smile that he reserves for customers and other people's parents.

"Good afternoon, ma'am. My friend and I are trying to earn money to go to Boy Scout camp this summer. If you would buy a few greeting cards from us, it would sure help a lot."

All the while he was talking, a little black dog scratched at the screen door and continued to bark at us.

The woman peered out the door above our heads, looking up and down the block as if she hoped to find some excuse to get out of the situation. I was right about her. She definitely wasn't eager to buy anything.

The woman glanced down at the dog. "Be quiet, Jasper!" she scolded.

"Rrraf!"

"What a cute little dog!" Rob said. "Would he mind if we petted him?"

The woman's face softened. "Oh, no, Jasper just loves to be petted. Don't you, Jasper?" she crooned. "You'd better come inside, then," she said to us, and opened the screen door a crack. "Jasper is such a naughty boy. He likes to run off, and then his mommy has a terrible time getting him back. Be careful now!" she warned, as we squeezed in. Jasper danced around our feet. "Don't let him get out!"

We both crouched down to pet the dog, who wriggled with pleasure.

"He sure looks smart," Rob said. "I bet he knows a lot of tricks."

"Well, Jasper does know how to stand up and beg for his dog yummies." The woman twittered.

Rob didn't waste much time before he socked her with the commercial message. "Would you mind looking at these a minute, ma'am?" he asked, holding up the box to her. "I'm sure there must be something here that you could use. Just a few orders would make all the difference to us."

The woman hesitated, but she could hardly make Rob continue to hold out the heavy box with one hand while he squatted there petting the dog with the other.

13

When finally she took the box from him, Rob grinned horribly at me and rolled his eyes up into his head. I tried to keep a straight face.

The woman opened the folder of stationery samples. "We-ll, maybe some informal notes . . ."

Rob smacked his knee, and the dog jumped back as if this was going to be a new game. "I knew you would pick those!" he crowed. "I could tell from your house that you had good taste." The woman looked pleased.

"Did you see the personal stationery that matches?" Rob asked. "You can have your name or initials printed free, any way you like."

"All right," she said. "I'll take a box of notes and a box of the letter size." Rob, who was still on the floor next to me, dug his elbow so hard into my ribs that I almost lost my balance.

"Here, just fill out how you'd like your name printed." Rob handed her a pencil and printed order form. "And, ma'am, while we're ordering, wouldn't you like a box of the all-occasion greeting assortment? When you buy them from us, they're ten cents cheaper a card than when you buy them at the store." He gave her another of those winning smiles.

She lowered her eyes, but she had to smile anyway. "My, you certainly are some salesman. All right, a box of cards, too."

Almost before the door had shut behind us, Rob and I both exploded with laughter. And we shoved each other all the way down the front walk.

"Boy, it's good we got out of there before I threw up!" I said. But I have to admit I really envied Rob's nerve. He actually enjoyed selling people stuff while I had trouble just getting some orders from my mother and grandmother and a few neighbors.

"What did I tell you?" Rob beamed. "Twelve more points. That makes 72 altogether."

A passing station wagon tooted at us. The tailgate was down and the back was crammed with garbage cans and brush. It was Rob's mother.

"Stop!" he yelled. "Where are you going?"

The car slowed down and stopped halfway down the block. His mother stuck her head out of the window. "I'm on my way to the dump," she said.

"Wait up, I want to come too!" Rob ran toward the car. "See you tomorrow, Mike," he said over his shoulder.

"Hey, you forgot your cards!" I called, but I guess he wasn't listening.

I didn't really care if we weren't going to sell cards any more that day. I didn't feel much like it anyway. But somehow I had the feeling of being left behind, too, while Rob ran off and did something else. This wasn't the first time, either.

chapter 2

I can always tell when it's Rob calling. So when the phone rang before school the next morning, I knew it was for me. My little brother, Morgan, always tries to beat me to it. I grabbed the receiver from him and said, "Hi, Rob."

"How'd you know it was me?" he asked.

"Who else calls up at the crack of dawn?"

"I'm starting a model club."

I had to hold my hand over my other ear because Morgan was screaming and trying to push me away from the phone.

"A what club?" I asked.

"A *model* club. You know, *models*—like rockets, planes, cars . . ." he explained impatiently. "We're going to build them in my garage."

"What does it have to be a club for? Why can't we just build models, like always?"

"With a club we could collect dues from everybody to buy supplies. And we can have model shows and give prizes for the best ones."

"Mike," my mother was asking, "are you taking your lunch today or buying it?"

17

"Taking," I answered over my shoulder. Morgan had finally shut up because my mother had given him a piece of toast with jelly, but he was yanking on the phone cord and getting it all sticky.

"Who's going to be in it?" I asked Rob, meaning the club. "The usual guys?" Rob is big on starting clubs.

"You, me, Bubba, and Andy. The first meeting's at my house after school. If anyone else wants to be in, they have to submit a model they made and we'll take a vote on it."

All the time he was talking, my mother was after me. "It's late. You'll be late, Mike. You're going to be seeing Rob in five minutes. Tell him you can talk about it at school."

But Rob was all excited. "My dad has an old showcase in his store. He said we can set it up in our basement to keep the models in."

Meanwhile I was holding Morgan off with my foot. He was laughing and trying to wipe jelly on me until he fell and banged his elbow. Then he started to scream again.

"Mike!" my mother yelled. "Will you please leave Morgan alone and get ready!" I always get the blame.

Rob was still talking. "Maybe we could charge admission. You could be the treasurer and keep track of the money. Or would you rather . . ."

"Listen," I interrupted. "I haven't eaten yet. I'll talk to you later."

Boy! Here we go, I thought, another club. Rob's clubs never work out, but you can't tell him that. The last one he started was a Nature Nick club, because his grandmother bought him a subscription to Nature

Nick magazine for his birthday and he was dying for an excuse to send for T-shirts and membership cards.

The club broke up after two meetings. Everyone was sick of Rob's telling them what to do. Besides, we weren't really too hot on nature, and nobody's parents wanted to fork out money for T-shirts. When Rob found that out, he lost interest in the club, too.

Our cafeteria is just the gym with some long tables and benches set up in it. It's as noisy at lunchtime as it is during a basketball game, only it smells different. By the time I got to the table where we usually sit, Rob had told Bubba and Andy about the club, and they were arguing already.

"Hey, Mike," Rob said, expecting me to back him up, "aren't we going to make models from scratch? Bubba wants to buy model kits."

Rob waited for me to agree with him, but I hesitated.

"Anyone can build from a dumb kit," Rob argued. "That's nothin'. The whole idea of the club is that we really build 'em."

I climbed over the bench into the last empty space, which was next to Rob. I looked sort of doubtful because, to tell you the truth, I had taken it for granted that we were going to use kits. That's what we always did.

Rob looked over at Andy. Andy just shrugged. "I like to build with kits. I don't see what's wrong with them," he said.

"Right!" Bubba added. "And I'm not going to be in the club at all if we can't use kits." He folded his arms and leaned his head to one side. I don't know which of us he was looking at because the windows of the gym were reflected in his glasses.

Rob was disgusted. He was used to having things go his way. But it made up my mind.

"I agree with Rob," I said. If it would make Bubba quit the club, I was all for building models out of toilet paper if I had to. His real name is Eliot, but Bubba is definitely not an Eliot. He's a Bubba. And when it comes to being Rob's friend, Bubba is my biggest competition.

Whenever Rob and I have a fight, he goes off with Bubba and leaves me flat. My little brother got really mad at me once when I let him down. "You're a flat-leaver!" he burst out. That's what Rob can be sometimes, a flat-leaver.

But Rob saw he wasn't going to have much of a club with just two of us.

"Okay." He backed down reluctantly. "Maybe we can have two classifications, kits and real models. Anyway, the first meeting is today at my house, right after school."

"Can't come. I have to go to the dentist. Ugh!" Bubba announced.

"I can't either," Andy said. "I've got drum and

bugle." Andy played in the Boy's Club band, and they were practicing for the Memorial Day parade.

Rob sighed. "All right. Tomorrow, then." When he makes up his mind to do something, Rob has to get started right away. He doesn't like to be held up for anything.

"Hey, could you shove over?"

It was Kenny. I'm afraid he's practicing to be my shadow. Now one wants Kenny to sit next to him because he never takes a bath. He really stinks!

Everyone pretended they didn't hear him.

"Hey, shove over. There's no room to sit down," Kenny whined.

Still, nobody moved.

"Shove over, will you? Lunch period's almost over!" Kenny was practically screaming. He's always in a panic about something.

I looked around. Everyone was either busy eating or else looking blank. I squeezed closer to Rob, and Kenny sat down next to me. At least it was better than having him eat across the table from me.

Kenny has a face like the giant grouper in the aquarium. He talks juicy, and it's worse when he has a mouthful. Even those big grouper lips can't close over his buck teeth.

"Aaak! What's that?" Bubba asked. He was staring at Kenny's lunch as if something was crawling out of the plastic wrap.

"Tuna fish and bean sprouts," Kenny answered, looking self-conscious. "It's good," he added, feebly.

"Tuna fish and bean sprouts. Oh, sickening!" Bubba pretended to puke on the table. Everyone snickered.

22

Bubba goes out of his way to put people down and his favorite target is Kenny because he's such an easy mark. When Kenny wears his basketball shorts under his clothes on gym day, Bubba always asks if it's because he doesn't want to undress in front of the guys, which Kenny doesn't. But that's nothing unusual—everyone kicks Kenny around. It's like he's there to pick on.

Bubba was cruising around the table now, looking for something more to eat. He slammed his fist down on my paper bag to see if it was empty. "You got any more in there?"

"Hey, cut it out!" I yelled. "Those are my cookies!"

"Cookies?" Bubba's eyes rolled comically, and he let his tongue hang out. "Oh, boy, cookies!" He started to open the bag.

"Get out of there!" I grabbed the bag and looked inside. The cookies were mostly okay.

Rob poked me with his elbow. "C'mon, Mike, so we can play kickball."

Kenny's ears perked up. "Hey, yeah, are we playing kickball?"

Rob groaned and said out of the corner of his mouth, "Hurry up. Let's go."

My peanut butter sandwich was stuck to the roof of my mouth, but it was too late to buy some milk to wash it down.

I got up from the table and shoved the bag with the other half of my sandwich in it toward Bubba. "Here, you want this?"

"Hey, yeah!" he said, snatching the paper bag.

24

I passed Rob some of the broken cookies, crammed the crumbs in my mouth, and palmed the rest.

"Okay, I'm finished," I said with my mouth full.

As we walked away, I heard Bubba swear.

"What's with him?" Rob asked, shoving all of the cookies into his mouth at once and looking back at the table.

I laughed. "Bubba's the only kid I ever heard of who doesn't like peanut butter."

chapter 3

After school I saw Rob by the bicycle rack frowning and looking for somebody in the crowd of kids.

"Where were you?" he wanted to know when he saw me. "I've been waiting here for an hour!"

"Wanna shoot some baskets?" I asked, jumping to sink an imaginary ball.

"Listen," he said, "I got some great stuff at the dump yesterday and I'm going to make a rocket out of it. Come on over and help me. It's going to be really neat!"

So that was where the idea for the new club had started—in the dump.

I shook my head. "We're going to do the model thing tomorrow. Let's play some basketball."

"Nah, I want to work on my rocket."

I didn't want to spend the rest of the afternoon in Rob's smelly garage, while he built his dumb rocket. He hardly ever comes to my house unless I've got something new to show him, and then he leaves right away. So when we got to the corner where I have to turn off for my street, I used one of his excuses. "My mother wants me home to baby-sit," I lied. "I'll see you."

"Okay, see you," he said, hurrying off. He didn't seem to care that much whether I came or not.

Boy, when Rob gets on one of these kicks, he's a regular fanatic! Do you know how many dumb ideas of his I've had to go along with or else he'd be mad at me?

Last Christmas he came over to ask if we had any ants.

"What do you mean, do we have any ants, for Pete's sake? We don't have any ants. What are you talking about?"

"I got this neat ant house from my grandmother," he explained, "but I have to order ants for it separately. It'll probably take weeks for them to come. Help me look for some."

"Rob, there aren't any ants this time of year," I said to him gently, like he was some kind of weirdo who might freak out when you broke it to him that there's no Santa Claus. "It's *winter*."

"Sure there's ants," he said, now that he was an expert. "What do you think happens to them? You can't have ants and then no ants. They're just hibernating. We'll dig them up."

So, guess what? We looked for signs of ants all over my front lawn, which is a mess of ant hills in the summer. You can't sit there without getting ants in your you-know-where. But I knew we wouldn't find even one. And we couldn't start digging around because the ground was frozen solid.

"What're you going to do with a box of ants,

anyway?" I asked. "You've got to get the queen, you know. If you don't get the queen, it won't do you any good even if you've got all the ants in the world."

"I'm going to put sugar in the box," Rob said. "That's what they like best. And we can watch them fight over it. It'll be neat!"

"Oh, sick!" I said in disgust. "That's what you've got me freezing my tail, crawling around the lawn for—an ant fight?" Sometimes Rob is really simple.

But it gave me my inspiration.

"Why don't we put some sugar out for bait? If there are ants here, they must be really hungry now. We can keep coming out and checking to see if they go for it."

Luckily, he liked my idea. And of course no ants ever showed up.

That's the only way I can ever get around Rob. I have to outsmart him. I can never win head on.

I don't know why I'm the one who always has to give in. Well, yes, I do know. As far as I'm concerned it's Rob or no one. He's been my best friend since we were six, even though we have our ups and downs.

There isn't anyone else. Kenny's a nurd, although I can take him in small quantities. Bubba is just a lot of noise. Andy's a nice kid, but he sticks pretty much to himself. The rest of the kids in my class come on the school bus, so they live too far away to be good friends. Or they're jocks. And the jocks really stick together.

When I got home, I checked the refrigerator. Nothing interesting, as usual. I took a drink from the container of milk. My mother would've hollered if she'd seen me doing that, but she wasn't around.

I was deciding whether the apples in the refrigerator drawer were already washed, when I heard somebody at the front door. It would be Kenny. His parents both work. There's never anybody home at his house, so he comes to mine all the time. That's why my mother says she's going to get a job, too.

He would have seen my bike out front, so I had to answer the door.

"Hi," I said, without any particular friendliness.

"Hi."

I just stood there, waiting, so he'd have to say why he was there. It wasn't very nice, but Kenny always brought out the worst in me.

His eyes traveled down to the apple in my hand. "Can I have an apple?"

I tossed it to him. He fumbled and dropped it. Then he followed me to the kitchen where I got another one for myself.

Kenny isn't so bad, really, but we don't have that much in common. Sometimes I try to ignore him when he comes over and go on perfecting my lay-ups or something. He doesn't seem to mind. He just watches me or plays with my brother Morgan's trucks. It never discourages him.

"You wanna go down to the paper store?" Kenny asked.

"No." I hate to say it, but I don't like the kids to see me that much with Kenny.

"I have money."

Kenny hangs around the newspaper store a lot. If I

go down with him, he'll buy us candy or baseball cards. Sometimes I even get a comic book. It's awful that he has to do that, just so he'll have a friend.

I think his parents give Kenny money to keep him out of their way. I guess I don't blame them much. Having Kenny around all the time can get on your nerves.

"I can't go today," I said.

"How come?"

"I told Rob I'd come over. I just stopped to tell my mother where I was going."

I don't know why I gave that as an excuse. It was the only thing I could think of.

Kenny is about my height, but his narrow chest and shoulders make him look crumpled up. And his parents always get his hair cut too short on the sides so he only has this little curly topknot. It makes him seem even more pitiful.

"Are you going to be in the club?" he asked.

"What club?" When you're on the spot, the best thing to do is play dumb. I didn't have the heart to tell Kenny he was going to be left out again. He looked so sad.

"Rob's club," he said. "*You* know. You're in it, right?"

"Uhh, yeah, I guess. Maybe. I don't know." Gee, why did Kenny always do that? I didn't want to hurt his feelings. It wasn't my fault Rob hadn't asked him to be in his club. I could see he didn't believe me.

I rarely paid enough attention to Kenny to notice that he actually had golden eyes. And when I did, like now, they always startled me. I had to look quickly away. Somebody was in those eyes, begging me to care about him.

To avoid that look, I said, "Okay, Kenny, I'll ride with you as far as the paper store."

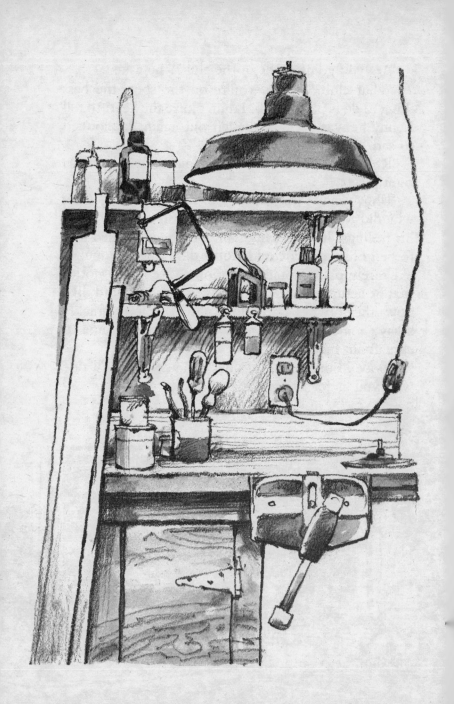

chapter 4

The workbench in Rob's garage was covered with scrap wood, broken toys, plastic egg cartons, wire, and plumbing parts. Rob was sitting on the garage floor, happily gluing two plastic bleach bottles together. He had cut the bottom out of the smaller one and set it on top of the larger one to make two stages of a slightly gross rocket.

"I see they've moved the town dump," I said, looking around at the mess.

"I thought you couldn't come over." Rob had that smug look he puts on when he thinks he's so smart or he's getting his way.

I pulled my baseball cap down over my eyes, tilted my head back and shrugged. "Yeah . . . well . . ."

Rob was trying to figure out how to attach the third stage of his rocket—an aerosol can—to the plastic bottles.

"There's a good movie at the Boy's Club this week," I said.

"Mmm." He had cut off the top half of the second stage bottle, but then he discovered he had to take them apart again in order to push the aerosol can through the second stage.

". . . *Frankenstein Meets the Moon Monsters*, or something like that," I continued. "It's got this neat part where they strap Frankenstein to this table, see. And they're going to dissect his brain. And they think he's out cold, so the guy goes over and. . . . Watch! You're not watching!"

Rob looked up.

"So this guy goes over to Frankenstein, and he reaches up and pulls down this buzz saw. And he's gonna saw off the top of his head, see. And Frankenstein goes . . . you're not watching!"

"I'm watching. I'm watching," Rob said, but he was wiping off the glue that was running down the bottles.

"Forget it." I gave up.

"How come you know what's going to happen?" Rob asked, wiping glue on his pants.

"I saw it already on TV. It's neat! I want to see it again."

I stood around and tried to think of something else to talk about, while Rob rummaged in the collection of junk on the workbench.

"My father said he might take me to a Red Sox game next weekend," I announced. Actually, I had asked Dad if he would take me and he had mumbled, "Maybe."

"Great," Rob said, pretending to be enthusiastic.

He glued five tops from spray paint cans to the bottom of the rocket, but the first three kept slipping off each time he started to add the next two.

"I'll hold the rocket up while you glue on the engines," I offered.

When the tops were glued on, Rob said, "Now hold it like that a minute."

He started drawing the fins on cardboard, measuring them against the rocket, erasing and redrawing them. I was getting stiff, squatting there.

"How long do I have to hold this?" I asked.

"Just a minute, okay? I'm going to paint it white. What color do you think I should make the stripe, red or black?"

"Black."

"Hmmm, maybe." He looked thoughtfully at the rocket. "I only have red, though. I think it'll look all right," he said, taping on the fins. "Would you get me a brush?" He nodded his head toward the shelves over the workbench.

"Aren't you going to wait till the glue dries?"

"It's dry enough," he said.

A skin had formed on the top of the paint in the can, but Rob stirred it up and started to paint the rocket. At first he carefully picked off the little lumps of paint skin and the hairs that kept coming out of the brush. Then he gave up on that.

"It won't show when I get all the details on," he explained.

We couldn't find another brush for the stripe. So when Rob painted it on with the same brush, the red got streaked with white.

"I never saw a rocket with pink stripes before," I said. "It's sweet."

"It needs a second coat," Rob announced huffily. "It'll be okay."

I was getting bored standing around, so I finally

decided to bring up the subject of Kenny. That always happens when I get bored; I generally do something I wind up sorry about later.

"Uh . . . Kenny found out about the club."

"So. Who cares?"

Rob can't stand Kenny. You should see what happens when one of them is at my house and the other one shows up. They act just like this dog, Rip, we used to have. When another dog came in our yard, Rip would stiffen up and try to decide whether he could chase him out or not. I guess three kids together never works, anyway. But when one of them is Kenny, he's sure to be the one who gets left out.

"Couldn't he be in it?" I asked.

"No, I don't want him in."

"He's not going to hurt anything. Come on."

Rob made a face. "Kenny always has to clown around. He's the only one who thinks he's funny."

"He's just trying to be one of the guys. When you get him alone, he calms down a lot. He's all right when he's at my house."

"Then *you* play with him. He's *your* buddy. Nobody else wants him around all the time like you do."

"He's not my *buddy*, Rob. I feel sorry for him. That's all. Just let him come to the meeting tomorrow, and if he makes any trouble you can kick him out."

"Okay," Rob grumbled, "but if he starts acting dumb, he's out. I mean it. He's out, period."

"Right. That's all I'm asking. Nobody ever gives him a chance."

To tell you the truth, I didn't really want Kenny in the club, either. But I couldn't stand his feelings being hurt. To jolly Rob up, I told him his rocket looked good. I have to admit it really was neat, except for the paint job. He was pleased.

"What do you think we ought to collect for club dues?" he asked. "Twenty cents a week? A quarter? Paint alone is going to cost a couple of dollars. Then we need glue and some new brushes. Do you want to be the treasurer or vice president?"

"What do you mean?" I asked, as if I didn't know. "Aren't we going to have elections?"

"No. It's *my* club," Rob said. "We're using *my* garage, right? And *my* father's tools. *I'm* the president. It's only fair."

"Fair! Fair is we have an election this time. You're always the president."

"Okay, okay," he said. "So we'll have an election if it makes you happy. It's all the same to me. I'll still turn out to be the president."

I would like to have said, "Maybe not this time," but I wasn't so sure about that. Somehow, Rob always got what he wanted. He had that smug look again, too. I felt like smashing him.

Rob's mother came out about then. She told us to clean up the mess and get it out of the garage so his father could park the car when he came home from work.

I put the lids back on the paint cans and Rob handed me the dirty brush.

"Here, put this back on the shelf and help me pick up the rocket," he said.

40

"How are we going to pick it up?" I asked. "It's still wet."

"So it's a little wet. We can't leave it here. My dad's going to drive right over it!"

I helped him pick up the sticky rocket so he wouldn't get hysterical. "Where are we going to put it?" I asked.

"In the basement."

It started to slump in the middle before we even got out of the garage.

"I told you to let the glue dry first," I said. "It's falling apart."

"No, it isn't," the rocket expert said. "Come on."

Rob never believes what I tell him. I could yell, "SHARK!" and he wouldn't come out of the water without giving me an argument.

Well, a couple of pieces fell off the rocket as we maneuvered around the basement doorway, but Rob said, "Don't worry. We'll get them later."

It was when I was backing down the basement stairs that the rocket did this slow cave-in.

When the glue gave way, stages two and three were jettisoned from stage one, which I was holding.

Rob yelled, "Get it! Get it!"

I tried to haul my end up by the engines because they weren't painted, but first the one in my right hand snapped off, then the other. Stage one bounced off my knee and down the basement steps.

"I told you to catch it," Rob said. "Now look at it. I can't glue it back together. The paint's all wrecked."

"Gee, I'm sorry, Rob." I tried to sound sincere because Rob was so burned, but I started to giggle.

"It just went *blughh*. . . ." To demonstrate, I collapsed on the stairs. And then I broke up laughing.

Rob didn't appreciate that, but the one who really got mad was my mother. I came home with paint on my new school pants.

I tried to tell her it wasn't my fault, that the rocket fell apart when I had to help Rob carry it. But she doesn't know how it is when you get involved in one of these things with Rob.

chapter 5

After school the next day all the guys who were going to be in the club met by the bicycle rack and rode over to Rob's house together. I told Kenny when I saw him in school that morning that he could come with us.

Rob had checked out everyone at lunchtime to make sure they would show up for the meeting so we could elect officers. I could swear he and Bubba were cooking up something together at recess. Rob had probably gotten Bubba to promise to vote for him, and then he was planning to make Bubba vice-president. I got the feeling that this club was going to turn out like all the others.

Rob's mother stopped us in the front hall before we got any further.

"Hey, guys, it's too nice a day to be inside," she said. "Why don't you have your meeting on the porch instead?"

She's always saying things like "Hey, guys." She tries to act like she's one of us. My mother would've just come straight out and said she'd cleaned the house and didn't want a bunch of kids in there messing it up.

Bubba beat everybody out to get the hammock. The rest of us took porch chairs except Rob, who leaned against the porch rail and faced us. He told everyone to pipe down. "Okay, does anyone want to nominate somebody for president?" I saw him give Bubba a look.

If Bubba was supposed to nominate Rob, and Rob nominated Bubba, Rob was sure to win.

"We don't have to have nominations," I said. "We don't have enough guys for that. Let's just have a secret ballot and everyone votes for the person they want."

Rob heaved a big sigh. Then as if he was doing me a big personal favor, he elaborately tore up a piece of paper from his notebook. We all used the same pencil so the ballots would look alike, and no one could tell who we voted for.

I figured out if I voted for myself, I could actually win with only two more votes. It was hard to tell who

Andy would vote for. I could probably get Kenny to vote for me. He was sitting there jiggling his knee like he had to go to the bathroom. When I caught his attention, I raised my eyebrows and pointed to myself. He frowned, giving me this I-don't-get-what-you're-saying look.

So I wrote my name on the slip of paper, shielding it with my hand, folded it into a little square, and hoped for the best.

I passed the pencil to Rob and watched him out of the corner of my eye as he wrote down a name. He seemed pretty confident. When everyone had finished, he collected all the slips of paper. Then he began to read off the names written on them:

"Rob. Bubba. Mike. Andy. Kenny."

It took a minute to sink into all our heads that everyone had gotten one vote. We all must have voted for ourselves! Then everyone tried to laugh, but I guess we were a little embarrassed. The problem was how to make the vote come out right the next time.

Bubba said, "We'll just make it a rule that nobody's allowed to vote for himself."

"How are you going to do that," I asked, "if you don't know who they voted for?"

"If it doesn't come out right next time, everyone will have to say how they voted," Rob explained. He was pleased because it looked like the voting thing was falling through.

"Yeah." Bubba agreed.

"Ve gif dem de truth serum," Kenny said, pushing Andy back in his chair and injecting his arm with an imaginary needle.

"Knock it off, Kenny." Andy brushed him away.

I knew if everyone had to admit who they voted for, they would all vote for Rob. Even I would probably vote for him then, or he'd be sore at me.

"Oh, no," I said to Rob. "A secret ballot is a secret ballot."

"A secret ballot is a secret ballot," mimicked Bubba in a squeaky voice. My voice gets a little high when I'm excited.

I gave him a dirty look.

Then Rob came up with another of his giant brainstorms. Each person would have to vote for two people. Then, even if you did vote for yourself, you would have to give someone else a vote, too. I couldn't see what the catch could be, so I agreed.

This time when we voted, I caught Kenny's eye again and fiercely jabbed my finger at my chest to show he should vote for me. He caught on and nodded.

It took a little longer for everyone to figure out how they were going to vote now. I put my name down first and then looked around at the other guys. I certainly wasn't going to vote for Rob or Bubba. Maybe Andy.

Andy's a nice kid. He never throws his weight around like Bubba. Yet he never gets picked on, even by the bigger kids who are always bugging us on the way home from school. He gets good marks, but nobody thinks of him as a brain. And he's good at sports. Still, I couldn't see him as president.

I finally decided to vote for Kenny. At least it would make him feel good to get a vote. He never got chosen for anything, except cleaning our table off at lunchtime.

Rob collected the ballots again and told Bubba to read off the names while he marked down the number of votes each of us got.

Bubba unfolded the little pieces of paper and read the names out one at a time.

"Rob, Kenny."

Rob had on his smug everything's-going-as-planned look.

"Mike, Kenny."

My chance to smile.

"Kenny, Mike."

My smile spread.

"Bubba, Kenny."

Gradually, both Rob and I stopped smiling. Kenny was getting an awful lot of votes. Nobody said a word. We just looked at each other, puzzled. Kenny was bouncing in his seat.

Bubba opened the last ballot.

"Andy, Kenny."

Kenny had won!

chapter 6

Kenny squealed and clapped his hands. He had been elected the president of one of Rob's clubs! Boy, I never heard of anything so funny in my whole life. Andy seemed to think it was kind of funny, too. But Rob was frowning.

Kenny, the dumb turkey, looked as if his team had captured the World Series. It was probably the biggest thrill of his life. He was too stupid to catch on that no one had really meant him to win. Everyone must have voted for themselves again. Then they had given their other vote to the person they thought would be the least competition—Kenny. Or they voted for Kenny because, like me, they felt sorry for him.

Kenny stood on a chair with his hand over his heart and started making a speech.

"My fellow Americans . . ." he began. And then in a deeper voice, "I want to thank you all for voting for a swell guy like me."

If he had been anyone else the other kids would have laughed and applauded, but nobody would give Kenny a break. They went on talking and ignored him. Rob and Andy were trying to see how hard they could hit each other with a foam rubber ball, and Bubba was tipping Kenny's chair with his foot.

Kenny tried to make everybody stop by calling the meeting to order. He finally succeeded in shutting them up when they saw he was really serious, but by then they had lost interest in the club. Every time he started to say something, Bubba would belch, which he could do at will, and crack us all up.

Then Kenny lost his temper, and it looked like he was about to cry. "Quit it, Bubba, or I'm going to punch you out!" he threatened.

Everybody had to laugh then. It was such a stupid thing for Kenny to say. Even though Bubba has more fat than muscle, nobody wants that ton of blubber leaning on them.

Bubba wasn't going to let it go by, either.

"What was that you said?" He put his hands on his hips and screwed up his face.

Kenny looked like a rabbit just about to be seized by some giant bird of prey.

"I just asked you to quit it, Bubba," he said, careful to keep his face and voice completely without expression.

"Or you're going to punch me out, right?"

I sucked in my breath. I didn't enjoy a slaughter.

"No," Kenny said, quietly. Luckily, he didn't have any pride to defend.

"What did you say?"

I saw Bubba check Rob to see how he was taking this. Now I understood why Bubba was always picking on Kenny. It wasn't just because Bubba was a

bully and Kenny was such an easy mark. Bubba
wanted Rob's approval.

Kenny cleared his throat. "I said *no*," he repeated
a little louder.

"That's better," Bubba said with satisfaction.

Rob grabbed Bubba by the arm.

"C'mon inside and help me get something to eat."

It was awkward, sitting on the porch, waiting for
Rob and Bubba to come back. Nobody said anything.
Thanks to Bubba, all the fun of Kenny's winning the
election had been spoiled. I avoided looking at
Kenny. I was afraid he might have started to cry.

I picked up the ball that had rolled under one of the
chairs and tossed it a few times.

"Hey, do you wanna play catch?" I asked.

Andy looked relieved at the chance to do something else and jumped up. Kenny needed a special
invitation.

"C'mon, Kenny," I called in his direction.

We had barely gotten off the porch when Rob and
Bubba came out with a box of crackers and some
American cheese.

Rob dealt it all out and then announced, while
appearing to study everyone's knees. "Uh, we can't
have the club anymore. My mother doesn't want so
many kids over at one time."

That wasn't cheese Rob was handing out. That was
pure baloney!

"Boy, Rob, you really have to have *everything* your
way, don't you," I burst out.

"What do you mean?" he asked, all innocence.

"Here I thought you got Bubba inside to cool him off," I said. "But you were just figuring how to weasel out of losing the election."

"That's not true. My mother said we were making too much noise. Ask Bubba. Right Bubba?"

"Yeah," agreed Bubba, the perfect witness.

I wasn't going to stay there and argue with either of them. They were really disgusting. I picked up my jacket and started off the porch.

"Hey, Andy," Rob said for my benefit. "Bubba and I are going to the Boy's Club to play pool. You wanna come?"

I turned and looked at Andy. He just stood there, embarrassed.

As I passed Kenny, he said, "Rob's being a sore loser. Right?"

"Oh, shut up, will you?" I muttered under my breath.

I headed toward the curb where we had left our bikes. But Kenny had gotten a taste of being in the center of things and he didn't want to give it up so fast. He went crazy, leaping off the porch rail and shouting, "Up, up, and away!"

I jumped aside so I wouldn't get clobbered. Instead of crashing into me, Kenny landed, *splat*, on the lawn. Everybody laughed because he looked so stupid, but Kenny had gotten back his audience. He pulled his arms out of the sleeves of his jacket and buttoned the collar around his neck.

"The caped crusader battles against the forces of evil!" he yelled, waving his arms. And then he

slammed his shoulder into me. I fell against my bicycle. As it went over, it tipped Rob's bike into the street.

Kenny lay giggling. I rubbed spit on my skinned elbow and said, "The forces of evil are going to leave tire tracks all over your chest."

From the porch, Rob yelled, "Hey, Mike! You knocked over my bike!"

"I did not!" Well, at least I hadn't meant to. It was Kenny's fault.

"You did so. I saw you."

"Big deal! It was an accident." Rob was really getting to be a pain.

"So pick it up."

"Pick it up yourself, Blob. I mean Rob."

This brought another burst of giggles from Kenny, who sank to his knees on the ground. The excitement of the day really must have been getting to him.

Rob's face was turning redder. Ordinarily, I would have picked up the bike. But it wasn't often that I got the best of Rob. I was feeling reckless and I wanted to get back at him for everything that had happened.

Two bigger kids came cruising down the street and saw us all standing around. They circled Rob's fallen bike like sharks and waited to see if there would be a fight.

A car was coming.

"You better hurry up, Blob. I mean, Rob," I sang out again. "Or you'll have a lot of little pieces to pick up later."

The driver of the car beeped his horn at us. The kids on bikes moved closer to the curb. Rob came roaring off the porch. I didn't know whether he was coming for the bike or for me. But I wasn't going to wait and find out so I picked up my bike and took off, chuckling to myself.

Halfway home I heard Kenny calling to me, "Hey, Mike. Wait up."

He rode up to me and said, "Wow, did you see how mad Rob was? He had to go and pick up the bike himself."

I just kept on riding like I didn't hear him. I wasn't in the mood for Kenny.

"You really got him this time," he said, trying to get me to talk to him.

I kept pumping the pedals and didn't say anything.

"Hey, Mike. Why don't we make our own club? We don't need Rob and Bubba."

"Kenny, what kind of a dumb club would that be, with only two guys in it?"

I never should have answered him because now he would never give up.

"Maybe we could get Andy," he said. "And Billy and Steve."

That would be just great, I thought. Billy and Steve were two jerky kids I've seen Kenny playing with sometimes. They were younger, too. I was beginning to wonder why I had started something. If Rob was going to be sore at me, all I would have left was good old Kenny and his kiddie friends.

"Look. Forget it, Kenny."

By this time we were in front of my house.

"Can I come in with you?" he asked.

"No, I don't feel like doing anything."

I was having trouble controlling my temper with him. If I hadn't been Mr. Nice Guy and gotten Kenny into the club, none of this would have happened. Now that Rob and I were mad at each other, I suppose Kenny figured this was his big chance to take Rob's place.

"We could look at TV," he suggested.

"Buzz off, will you, Kenny!"

He got this look on his face like he'd suddenly become an orphan, and then he slowly rode away without saying anything else.

That's Kenny. He brings it on himself, and then he gives you this hurt act so you're supposed to feel sorry and call him back to apologize. It usually works on me, but it didn't this time. I was too busy feeling sorry for myself.

chapter 7

That night was the movie at the Boy's Club. Rob always comes by my house so we can go to the show together. It didn't occur to me until it got late that maybe Rob wouldn't show up. I waited as long as I could. When he still didn't come, I had to run all the way so I wouldn't miss the beginning.

I felt kind of self-conscious going in alone. I never had before. The picture hadn't started, but the lights were going off. There's always a big crowd for horror movies, so there was only one seat left, and it had a jacket on it. I picked it up and sat down.

"Hey! That's mine."

I turned around. Wouldn't you know? Bubba had to be in the seat behind me. But my annoyance changed to hurt when I saw Rob sitting next to him.

"Where's your friend Kenny?" Bubba asked.

Rob was wearing his silly expression.

I tried to come up with a clever answer. There's no way to get back at Bubba, though. Even if you've got some really great comeback for one of his remarks, it goes right over his head.

Luckily, the movie started then. It's always noisy at

the club movies, and during a horror picture the kids scream and laugh a lot. But all through the first half I could hear Rob and Bubba whispering. I knew they were talking about me.

A couple of times someone kicked my chair. Whenever I turned around and looked, either Bubba or Rob would ask, "Is something the matter?" And when I turned back to the movie again, they would start to snicker.

Then Bubba slid way down in his seat so he could stick his feet between the back and the seat of my chair. He kept nudging me in the rear.

I turned around and said, "Take your big feet off my chair, will you?"

And he said with great politeness, "Oh, sorry."

I didn't want to give them the satisfaction of making me move, and besides, there weren't any other seats. Even if I felt like standing in the back, I would have to climb over the whole row of kids to get to the aisle. I decided to stick it out and then move after intermission.

Most of the kids went upstairs during intermission because there was a pool table and refreshments up there. I got a soda from the machine and stood looking around. Rob was at the snack counter saying something to Bubba, but he was looking at me. A minute later Rob came over and pretended to accidentally bump my elbow so my soda would spill.

"Hey, what did you do that for?"

I was brushing the soda off my pants when someone came up behind me and grabbed my baseball cap. I spun around and saw Bubba with his hands behind his back.

"Cut it out, Bubba. Give it back!"

They both knew how much that cap meant to me. It was my trademark. I almost never took it off. My father went to school with this guy who's a coach for the Red Sox. We went to a game once and my father took me down to the locker room after it was over. That's when the coach gave me my Red Sox cap. For weeks all I talked about was that game and what it was like being in the team's locker room.

Bubba threw the cap to Rob. Rob looked at it and said, as if he didn't know, "Is this the one you got from your friend the coach? Let's see if he autographed it for you."

I ran over to Rob, but he laughed and tossed the

cap back to Bubba. Bubba threw it over the pool table to another kid, who stuck it under his arm and made an imaginary touchdown. I pushed through the groups of kids who were standing around, but as soon as I got close to the one with the cap, he would pass it to someone else.

More kids caught on to what was happening. They started stomping and cheering and calling to the guy with the cap to throw it to them.

Then Rob hooked the cap from under someone's arm and plopped it backwards on his own head.

"Come on. That's enough Rob," I begged. But all the kids were egging him on, and he was looking around at them, grinning.

"Okay." My voice started to break. "You win. Now give me back the cap. *Please!*"

I tried to snatch the cap off his head, but he grabbed it first and made a run for the door. He had to slow down when he got to the stairs, and I caught him by the shirt. There was a tearing sound so he stopped. But he still held on to the cap, crouching over it with his back to me so I couldn't get at it. I pounded on his back with my fists, yelling through my clenched teeth, hitting him with each word.

"Give . . . me . . . the . . . cap! *Rob!* Give it to me!"

He hunched against the wall and howled, "Ow! Ow!" but he was laughing, too, which made me even angrier. When he realized I wasn't holding his shirt any more, he stumbled down a few steps with me right behind. I grabbed his arm and tried to reach the cap, but he switched hands and threw the cap over the railing.

Downstairs, the kids were filling the narrow hallway as they went back to their seats. Except for one guy who looked up after he was hit by the falling cap, no one saw it and it was trampled underfoot.

That really did it. I was going to get Rob for this!

Up until now, Rob and I had never had a real fight. I'm not exactly a fighter, anyway, and Rob is more likely to get Bubba to do his fighting for him. But this time I really let him have it. I didn't even care about getting hurt myself.

Let me tell you, it isn't easy fighting on stairs. There isn't much room either. I shoved against Rob to keep my balance. Grabbing his collar with one hand, I kept banging his head against the wall with the other. The blood was pounding in my own head. My face and ears were burning and, to my shame, I started crying like a dumb baby.

Rob tried to push me off and he got down another step. Now all I could really manage was to hit him on the head and shoulders. He must have been surprised at how mad I was because he didn't really fight back. He just tried to protect his head with his arms. That's probably what threw him off balance.

When I saw that I wasn't getting anywhere just pounding him with my fists, I gave him a tremendous shove. Immediately, I realized my mistake. I reached out to grab him back, but it was too late. He went crashing down the steep flight of stairs.

I'll never forget seeing him fall. It seemed to take forever, like slow motion in a movie. Horrified, I shut my eyes and held my breath. I was afraid I had killed him.

chapter 8

The noise and the horsing around that always goes on during intermission stopped. All you could hear was the shuffling of feet upstairs in the poolroom. It was as though the movie we were part of had been stopped at the point when everyone was looking at us.

Sam, the club's director, shoved his way through the crowd in the hallway. I heard a kid telling him that I had pushed Rob. Sam squatted down and took Rob's hand away from where he was holding his head. I couldn't tell how much he was hurt from where I was on the stairs. Sam examined Rob's face and talked to him very quietly. I saw Rob nod his head.

Then Sam stood up and brushed off his pants and said, "Okay, the rest of you kids go back to your seats. The movie is going to start."

Then he glared up at me. "I told you boys never to fool around on these stairs."

Sam helped Rob to his feet. "Come on, Rob. Let's take care of that eye." Rob seemed to be walking okay. Bubba followed him and Sam into the bathroom across the hall.

I stood on the stairs feeling light and trembly like when you first get off a roller coaster. Aren't they going to do anything to me? I wondered. What was supposed to happen now?

The kids who had been upstairs missed the fight.

"Hey, who got hurt?" someone behind me asked.

I pretended I didn't know he was talking to me.

"Somebody fell down the stairs," I heard another kid answer.

I was ashamed to admit what I had done. I had the feeling they would all be on Rob's side. So I tried to get lost in the crowd and hurried downstairs.

I saw where my cap had been kicked into a corner of the hall. It was all dirty and the visor was bent. I picked it up and got out of there as fast as I could.

It was better outside in the darkness; cool and quiet. It's funny—I suddenly realized I wasn't angry any more. I mean I was still mad at Rob and Bubba for bugging me, but I didn't *feel* angry. You know? I guess they had gotten to me mostly because it was the two of them, together. I hadn't really thought about what I was doing when I pushed Rob. But, oh, boy, when I saw him falling down those stairs, I was scared!

When I got home, my parents were in the living room watching TV.

"Hi," my mother called, looking up from the set.

"Hi."

I hurried past without looking at either of them on my way upstairs.

"How was the movie?" my father asked.

My voice must have come out sort of squeaky because my mother knew right away that something had happened.

"Mike, is something the matter?" My mother's a regular bloodhound when something funny's going on.

Halfway upstairs, I called back, "No . . . well, Rob and I had a fight. That's all." I was beginning to tremble all over, and I was afraid I couldn't hide it. I wanted to get to my room and crawl under the covers.

"A fight? What happened? Come back here, Mike. You mean a real fight, or just an argument?"

"Rob and Bubba kept bugging me and bugging me. And I just couldn't take it any more."

I wasn't going to tell her about pushing Rob. She would give me a lecture about how I had to control my temper, how people could get hurt that way. I already knew all that, the hard way.

"Well, is everything all right now?" she asked.

"Sure . . . fine."

I made it up to my room before she thought of any more questions. I got ready for bed and then started going through my stacks of old comic books, trying to find one I hadn't read in a while. But I couldn't get interested in them. I kept thinking about the fight and wondered how Rob was. But I was afraid to call him. I'd have to say I was sorry, too, and I wasn't. Maybe I was sorry if he was hurt, but I wasn't sorry about the rest. He had asked for it. Besides, my mother would hear me and want to know what was going on. Maybe *his* mother would answer. I didn't want to talk to *her*. She'd really be mad that I'd hurt her darling boy.

Was that the phone? Yes. Maybe Rob was calling to say he was sorry. I jumped off the bed and bumped my head on the top bunk. Wow! You really do see stars. My door always sticks, and I had to pull at it a couple of times before it would open.

My mother was talking to someone. What if it was Rob's mother, telling my mother the whole thing! I went to the head of the stairs and listened. My heart was thumping.

My mother was doing all the talking, but I couldn't hear what she was saying. Then she laughed about something. "Ted," she called to my father, "the Carrolls want to know if we'd like to have dinner with them Sunday night."

I let out a deep breath. Boy, what a relief! Then I

70

went back to my room, fished out the last piece of bubble gum from the top drawer of my dresser . . . and stopped. That phone call had done it. I couldn't hide upstairs in suspense, waiting for something to happen. It was better to get it over with. I went down and dialed Rob's number.

"Hello?" His mother answered so fast that I wasn't prepared.

"Uh . . . C–could I s–speak to Rob?" I stuttered, breaking out in a cold sweat, even though my bare feet on the kitchen floor were freezing. I shifted my weight and tried to warm one icy foot against the back of the other knee.

"He's not here, Mike."

"He's not?"

"He's sleeping over at Bubba's."

Bubba's! I never figured on his doing that.

"Do you want him to call you tomorrow?" she asked.

I tried to sound ordinary. "No, thanks. I'll see him around. 'Bye."

No thanks! That rat! Here I was worried about him, thinking I should say I was sorry. Sorry! I was sorry I hadn't pushed him harder. Boy!

I flopped down on my bed again and remembered how Rob and Bubba had gone out of their way to make me look like a jerk. I tried to think what they might be doing at Bubba's right now. It was hard. I could never imagine what they *ever* did together. Bubba was so dumb.

The best times Rob and I had were when we slept at each other's house. Even when we had to go to bed, we would lie awake for hours talking. I would say how I felt about things, things I never told anybody else, and I could tell Rob really understood.

Like the time this girl in our class, Mary Ann, kept sending me notes, and I secretly thought she was neat. I didn't want to admit it because we both agreed we hated girls; they were always giggling and acting dumb. But Rob didn't laugh at me when I told him. He said he liked her, too.

We talked about what we wanted to be when we grew up. I thought I ought to know, but I didn't. We were really close then. It was never the same during the day. Rob became a different person, especially if there were other kids around.

How could Rob ever be that close to someone like

Bubba? What did he see in Bubba anyway? Whenever I asked Rob how he could stand him, he always said, "Oh, Bubba's all right." I stuffed my head under the pillow and groaned. It was going to be some dumb summer!

I tried to think about something else, but it didn't work. It was going to be like that time when Rob was sick and didn't come to school for two weeks. That was the trouble with having a friend. You got used to doing everything together, and nothing was the same when he wasn't around.

Baseball practice was tomorrow. Rob and Bubba would be there. Everywhere I went, they would be there. And I would be all by myself.

Finally I must have fallen asleep, because the next thing I knew my mother was shoving me and telling me to hurry and have some breakfast before I went to practice.

The last thing I felt like doing that Saturday morning was hurry.

chapter 9

On the way to the field I saw Kenny. He was sneaking around the side of his garage with Billy Martin, wearing a little kid's plastic helmet and carrying a rifle made out of scrap lumber. Our ex-president. "President for a Day"; it would make a good TV show. I whizzed by on my bike without slowing down, but Kenny saw me.

"Hey, Mike!"

"I got practice," I yelled over my shoulder. Thank goodness Kenny didn't go in for sports. It was one way to get rid of him for a while.

"Rob's over at Bubba's," he shouted.

You can always count on Kenny to pass along bad news. When I got to the field, Rob and Bubba were both there already, running their five warm-up laps around the track.

"Mike!" the coach called. "Late again? Do an extra lap."

I swore under my breath and threw down my glove. The rest of the kids began to break up into two groups as they finished their laps. The first string took their positions in the infield.

Bubba was the only runner left and he had worked up a sweat. His glasses were fogging up. If it was me chugging around all that blubber, I would probably be getting razzed. But Bubba was a strong hitter, so he got respect. The only satisfaction I had was in sprinting easily past him on my way around the track.

After I did my laps, I trotted over to the outfield where Fred, the assistant coach, was hitting balls to my group. He was hitting them pretty hard. A couple of kids were already doing extra laps for missing theirs. I found a place to stand where I could watch Rob out of the corner of my eye.

Rob had his new cleats on. I was watching him retie the laces so he could call attention to them when I realized Fred was yelling at *me*.

"You want to try for the next one, Mike . . . *after* you finish another lap?"

A couple of kids were grinning at me, and some were looking behind me on the ground. I turned around and there was the ball lying about twenty feet back.

When we switched to infield practice, I tried to pay more attention to what was going on. But I was finding it hard to concentrate. I was still half asleep and I kept looking over at Rob to see what he was doing.

The coach was hitting balls to each of the basemen. We had to make the play to whatever base he told us to. He started off with me on third.

"Play it to first," he called.

He really had it in for me that day, because his first hit was a line shot down third base. I had to backhand it and throw it to first.

I could swear it was Rob who called over, "Nice stop!"

But the coach yelled, "Next time cut out the fancy stuff and be out there in front of the ball!"

He was always teed off about something. Probably it was because we were last in the league. We really stank. But even if you did something that turned out right, he had to find something wrong with it.

I looked over at Rob on second base. Had he really said, "Nice stop"? But he was already watching the coach, waiting for his grounder. His eye was swollen some, but I figured it must be all right if he was playing.

When everyone was called in for the scrimmage,

the coach divided us up into teams. Rob and I wound up on the same side. He was on second base. I was on third. Bubba was catching and Andy played the outfield on the other team. He had a good throwing arm.

We were up first. I avoided the dugout where Rob and Bubba were sizing up everybody as they came up to bat. I just stood in the doorway watching the game and pretending not to notice them.

Coach came up to me and said, "Get a helmet, Mike. You're on deck. I want you to bunt. If you don't make it the first time, look at me. If I slap my knee, try it again. If I touch the brim of my cap, forget it."

I picked out a bat, slipped on the donut and took

some practice swings. I saw the kid ahead of me jogging to first. He must have gotten walked. The batter's box was empty. I could feel Rob and Bubba watching me and I was afraid it would make me goof.

Someone called out, "C'mon, Mike. Park it first pitch."

And then I heard nearby, "Don't count on it."

I recognized *that* voice. Bubba.

The pitcher kicked some dust and started his wind-up. First pitch was right in there. I squared away to bunt. The ball hit the top of my bat and fouled off. The catcher flipped off his mask and gloved the easy pop. I tossed my helmet, dropped the bat, and walked to the dugout. As I passed, Bubba called out.

"Nice hit."

And I heard the snickers.

Bubba was on deck now. The next batter stepped up and got a base hit. Bubba walked to the plate and took some slow practice swings. I made a few silent prayers that weren't answered, because I heard the crack as he connected. I saw Andy in center field, chasing the ball. That would have made for three easy bases, but since Bubba is slow, he only got two. The guy on first made it home. The next batter hit a pop fly for the second out.

Rob was up next. He knocked some nonexistent dirt off his cleats with the end of his bat. The first ball came in on the outside for a strike. Rob just looked at it like it wasn't his style. He stepped out of the box and readjusted the strap of his batting glove.

The next ball came in pretty fast. I saw Rob shut

his eyes when he swung. Rob isn't such a good ball player, but he sure is lucky. The ball dropped safe in right field, giving him a base hit.

After the next out, we took the field. Our pitcher got off to a slow start, as the first two batters collected base hits. Their next batter flied out to right field, but the runners advanced one base anyway. That put runners on second and third.

The next pitch was kind of wild. The man on third didn't move, but the man on second jumped the gun.

The coach yelled, "Get back! You can't run! There's a man on third!"

Everyone laughed, and it broke the tension.

The next hit was a line drive over my head. I jumped up and felt the ball carry my glove backward. I prayed I wouldn't drop it. I glanced over and saw that the second base runner had stopped dead in the middle of the base lines and Rob was right behind him. I winged it to Rob, and he tagged the guy out. We'd made a double play!

Rob was grinning at me, and it made me feel great. I grinned back. Boy, he had a beautiful black eye! I'm not sure . . . I think we finally lost the scrimmage. But for me, the game went better after that.

After practice I hung around the field hoping Rob would come over to me and say something. He seemed to want to forget about the fight, and I did, too. Finally I got up the courage to walk over to the fence where Rob was getting his sweat jacket.

"How's your eye?" I asked.

"It's okay," he said, trying to act cool. But then he

added proudly, "You should have seen it last night. It was all puffed out. I could hardly see!"

"Rob," I said, feeling uncomfortable, "I'm sorry. I didn't really mean to push you."

He shrugged like it didn't matter, but he didn't say he was sorry, too, about what *he* had done.

"Hey, do you want to go around with the samples again today?" I asked. I thought I would suggest something he'd like to do.

Rob's face brightened. "Yeah, okay—we're going to have to hustle to get 350 points."

"Why 350?"

"To get the BB gun," he said, as though I knew what he was talking about. Bubba came over then and stood behind Rob, tossing a ball in the air and taking in our conversation.

"You'll never get 350," I said. "It'll take all year."

"No, it won't. We've already got over 70, and that's almost a quarter of what we need."

"But half of it's mine, if we're partners. I thought we were going to divide the points and each of us pick out something."

"Nah," Rob said, putting down the idea. "The rest of the stuff in that catalog is junk."

It was the first I'd heard about it.

"You can use the gun whenever you want," he promised generously. "I'll just be keeping it at my house, that's all."

Bubba laughed.

"How about keeping it at *my* house and you can use it whenever *you* want." I shot a look at Bubba and remembered this time to keep my voice from getting squeaky.

"Look, I sold most of the stuff," Rob argued.

My mouth opened, but I didn't say another word. I just turned my back on him and Bubba and walked away.

chapter 10

I didn't want Bubba and Rob to see me going home by myself. So when Andy dumped the bat bag in the trunk of the coach's car and started to leave, I called after him, "Hey, Andy, wait up!"

He stopped and turned around. "What's up?"

"Nothing. I'll walk you."

I pushed my bike along next to him, and we walked down the street without saying anything much until we came to my house.

I didn't want to ask him in. I knew how it would be because he'd come over a few times before. A big zero. It's not that I don't like Andy. We just don't know what to do when we're together. We don't click.

"I'll see you," I called over my shoulder as I hopped on my bike and glided up my walk.

"Yeah. See you, Mike."

When I came into the house, my mother was vacuuming the living room. She glanced at me over her shoulder and said, "Why so glum? Lose the game?"

"It wasn't a game, Mom. It was just practice."

"Well, whatever. What's the matter, then? Have another fight with Rob?"

"No, I had a nothing with Rob. I have nothing with nobody. That's just it. I don't have anybody. I haven't got any friends, at least not anybody I care about."

"Oh, Mike! What are you saying? You have lots of friends."

She really didn't understand, and it would have been a waste of time trying to explain. I stomped upstairs to my room.

My mother shut off the vacuum and called up the stairs, "Mike?"

"What?"

"It will blow over, and you and Rob'll be back together in a few days."

I came down the stairs again and flopped in a chair. My mother leaned on the vacuum, studying me, but I looked past her at the wall.

"Why don't you call Rob and invite him over for dinner?" she suggested.

"No, I don't want to. Anyway, he probably wouldn't come."

"Sure, he would. Tell him if he comes I'll make a pizza."

"Look, Mom," I yelled at her. "You don't get it! He does this to me all the time!" I was close to tears. "He's always got to run things."

"Do you want to run things?"

"No, but just once in a while I'd like to have it my way. Just once!"

"I know, Mike. But you can't change Rob. He is the

way he is. You have to decide whether his friendship is worth it."

"Some choice!" I said.

Morgan came in with a toy car and a handful of tires he had taken off the wheels.

"Dese came off," he said, handing them to my mother.

She took them and then turned back to me. "Don't worry," she said. "Some day you'll meet someone else, maybe in high school, who will be your idea of a friend."

"But Mom, I don't want to wait until then. What am I supposed to do *now*?"

Morgan shoved at my mother's legs. "Fix it! Fix it!"

She sat down and tried to pull the tires over the rims. Then she looked at me again.

"Mike," she said gently, "you can't depend on other people to make your life for you. That isn't what friends are for."

That sounded good, I thought. But as far as I was concerned, having a friend was everything.

My mother struggled some more with the tires and then handed them back to my brother.

"Look, Morgan. Mommy can't fix them right now. She's talking with Mikey. I'll try later."

"No. Now!" he pleaded, stamping his foot.

"Later," she said calmly.

He threw himself on the floor and burst into tears.

"Why don't you go in the kitchen and see if you can find the box of cookies in the big paper bag," she said to him, ignoring the tantrum. "I'll be there in a minute to pour you some milk."

"Okay," he said, the fake tears over at once.

"Would you like some, too?" she asked me.

I shook my head slightly and got up. As I passed her chair on my way upstairs again, she reached for my hand. She squeezed it and gave me a reassuring smile. It only made me feel worse.

I went up to my room and started playing some of the tapes Rob and I had made of our favorite songs on the radio. We used to sit up half the night waiting for a particular record to be played.

I looked out the window and down the empty street. The cool glass felt good against my forehead. I remembered Ryan back in kindergarten. He had been the kind of friend I wanted. It was funny, I couldn't picture any more what Ryan looked like, except that he had yellow hair.

But I was a little kid then. It was different now. I wasn't going to find a friend like that so easily. Maybe I had made a friend out of Rob just because I was lonely. But it must have been more than that because we'd been friends for a long time.

Suddenly my scalp prickled. I heard voices downstairs and then the familiar thump, thump, thump of Rob's big feet running up the stairs.

"Mike?" he called through the door.

"Yeah?"

Rob turned the handle, but the door stuck. He shoved against it while I pulled on the handle. The sticking door gave way and banged against my toe as Rob crashed in.

"I see you got your door fixed."

He caught my eye and we both laughed until embarrassment made us look away. I sat down on the bed and stared at the tape recorder on the floor, tapping my foot and nodding my head as if I was listening to the song that was playing. But my stomach felt shaky. What was I supposed to say? What had Rob come to say to me?

He was still standing in front of the bed. A paper bag under his arm crackled each time he shifted his weight.

"I see you got your cap back," he said, looking up on the bedpost where it had been hanging since the night before.

"Yeah, but I can't wear it any more," I said bitterly.

"I'm sorry that happened to it," he said, and I could see he meant it, too. Then he reached into the bag. It was from The Sport Shop on Main Street.

I knew what was in there—a new cap. He'd bought me a cap to show how he felt. The knot in my stomach melted and a warm glow spread out through my arms and legs. Rob was really a good guy.

"Look what I got." He took out a new green and white batting glove and put it on, stretching it smoothly over each of his fingers and tightening the strap around his wrist.

"How does it look?" he asked. Rob grabbed my bat and took a few swings with it in front of my dresser mirror.

"Okay," I said, feeling confused. The glove was for him?

"I left my other one in the dugout and somebody swiped it."

I lay down on the bed with my hands behind my head and looked at the rusty springs under the top bunk. I was trying not to let him see my disappointment.

That's Rob, I thought. My mother was right. He never was going to change. He thought my cap didn't mean any more to me than his old glove.

"You wanna take the cards around?" he asked. "We'll split the points like you said."

"I thought everything in the catalog was just junk," I said.

"I only said that."

"Why don't you sell cards with Bubba?"

"He's riding around on his brother's trail bike. That's all he ever wants to do."

Now *I* was replacing *Bubba*. For the first time I realized that it wasn't just *Bubba* I had to worry about. There would always be someone else whenever Rob didn't get his way. Everything was easily replaced . . . even friends.

"Maybe you should be more particular about your friends," I said spitefully.

"Maybe you're too particular."

Maybe you're right, I thought. Maybe that's my trouble.

"Well, do you want to sell cards, or don't you?" he asked.

"To tell the truth, Rob, I don't really want to sell cards, either," I said slowly.

He shrugged. "Okay."

The tape came to an end, and I swung off the bed to change it.

"Do you still have that disc jockey tape we made?" Rob asked.

"I think it's on this one," I said, putting another tape on.

There was a hum, some giggles in the background and then Rob's voice rasped, "This is Sly Brucie on station WWR, ra-dee-o, playing the best in pops. Here is the number one song this week, by the O-rang-u-tans!"

Rob laughed, and the sound of his laugh was so infectious, I had to chuckle, too.

Then a rock group came on, played at half speed, so they sounded like they were moaning from the bottom of a well. They were interrupted by me, speaking in a high voice, phoning in a request for my boy friend's favorite song.

I remembered the day we made that tape. Rob's parents were away for a week and he was staying with us. It was like having a brother. I mean a real one, not just a pest like Morgan.

"Where's the one we did about 'Witchy-poo'?" Rob asked.

Witchy-poo was our private name for Miss Thorsten, the math teacher. She wasn't old or ugly or anything, but it wouldn't take much for her to be a witch. It came naturally.

I pushed the fast forward button and then play, until I heard myself as Miss Thorsten shrieking at Rob. Then I pushed the reverse button and started it at the beginning.

Rob and I sat on the rug listening and laughing, until my mother called up the stairs.

"Rob, your mother wants you home, right away."
We both groaned. I didn't want him to go so soon.
"Hey, why don't you come over for dinner tonight!" I suggested, while he pulled hard at the door.

"Sure, I'll call you later," he said over his shoulder

as he left. He didn't even check first to find out what we were having.

I sat there by myself till the tape ran out. Somehow all the bad stuff that had happened between Rob and me in the last few days didn't seem that important any more. I felt happy about things for a change. I knew it wasn't going to last—Rob would still make me mad sometimes. But I wasn't going to expect him to be someone he wasn't. It was enough that we were still friends.

Then I picked up my basketball and went downstairs, spinning the ball on my finger. I only dropped it twice, and then dribbled it through the kitchen, even though it's against house rules.

Outside, I threw the ball over a low-hanging branch, scoring an imaginary point.

ABOUT THE AUTHOR AND ILLUSTRATOR

CAROL AND DONALD CARRICK are the well-known author and illustrator of many fine books for children. Among their Clarion titles are *Octopus, Sand Tiger Shark,* and the series of stories about Christopher, starting with *Sleep Out* and including *The Accident, The Foundling* and *The Washout.*

In the winter the Carricks live on Martha's Vineyard with their two sons, Christopher and Paul, and in the summer the family moves to a cabin in the woods in northern Vermont.